THE
BOOK
of
COOL

Cool Questions. Cooler Answers.

THE BOOK of COOL

Cool Questions. Cooler Answers.

Tim Wesemann

Illustrated by
Artmasters

Zonder**kidz**

Zonder**kidz**.

The children's group of Zondervan

www.zonderkidz.com

The Book of Cool
Copyright © 2004 by Tim Wesemann

Requests for information should be addressed to:
Grand Rapids, Michigan 49530

Library of Congress Cataloging-in-Publication Data

Wesemann, Tim, 1960-
    The book of cool : cool questions, cooler answers / by Tim Wesemann.-- 1st ed.
        p. cm.
    ISBN 0-310-70696-3 (pbk.)
    1. Boys — Religious life — Miscellanea — Juvenile literature. [1. Conduct of life. 2. Christian life.]
I. Title.
    BV4541.3.W47 2004
    248.8'–dc22

                                        2003026123

Editor: Gwen Ellis
Interior design: Chris Tobias
Art direction: Michelle Lenger

Printed in the United States of America

04 05 06 07 /❖DC/ 10 9 8 7 6 5 4 3 2

To the coolest of the cool . . . Jesus Christ
and to three of his coolest kids:
Sarah (ladies first, gentlemen), Christopher, and Benjamin.
I love you!
-Tim Wesemann

Dedicated to my Mom, Grandma, and Grandpa
for teaching me that it is good to be cool,
but even cooler to be good.
-Graham Smith

What is  SOUL GEAR ?

Based on Luke 2:52:
"And Jesus grew in wisdom and stature,
and in favor with God and men" (NIV).

2:52 is designed just for boys 8-12!
This verse is one of the only verses in
the Bible that provides a glimpse of Jesus
as a young boy. Who doesn't wonder what
Jesus was like as a kid?

Become smarter, stronger, deeper,
and cooler as you develop
into a young man of God
with 2:52 Soul Gear™!

Zonderkidz

The 2:52 Soul Gear™ takes a closer look by focusing on the four major areas of development highlighted in Luke 2:52:

"Wisdom" = mental/emotional = **Smarter**

"Stature" = physical = **Stronger**

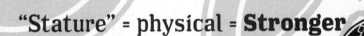

"Favor with God" = spiritual = **Deeper**

"Favor with men" = social = **Cooler**

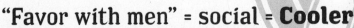

Introduction

It's so cool to be able to write a book especially for boys who are not only growing in their faith, but also growing in their relationships with others. Yes, that's you! Just like Jesus became wiser and stronger, he also grew in favor with God his Father, and with others. That's so cool!

In learning to deal with other people, we need to know what's cool and what's not. That's the idea behind *The Book of Cool!* It includes stuff like using good manners (I know, it sounds blah, but they're needed), living our faith in the world, and learning to live with families, our friends, and ourselves. The book is written in a question and answer format.

To find answers to those questions, we'll get help from the coolest book ever — the Bible. Many of our answers will come from the book of Proverbs in the Old Testament. It is filled with wise words for the cool at heart! Obviously, you won't find direct answers to every question you might ask in the Bible, especially when so many of the things we have questions about today weren't invented back then. Paul didn't email his letters, in case you wondered!

There's another cool thing about the book of Proverbs. Many times a chapter or section in the book of Proverbs begins with the words, "My son . . ." It is like getting a letter that shares God's wisdom. That's *so* cool! Now I have that opportunity to write to you in order to share God's wisdom. So, my sons . . . get ready as together we learn what's cool and what's not.

Many thanks to Zonderkidz and my editor, Gwen Ellis, for honoring me with this project. Special thanks to family and friends who offered up prayers along with ideas and words of encouragement!

Stay cool in Christ, my friends!

— Tim Wesemann

IS IT COOL to Win the "Gross-Out" Competition at Recess?

So, you won the Gross-Out Competition at school recess? You must be *so* proud. I'm sure your parents must be happy for you too! (I wonder what a first-place gross-out trophy would look like?)

One of the key points here is that it happened "at recess." And that's okay. It wouldn't be cool to win a gross-out competition at your aunt's wedding or at your cousin's graduation party or while your youth group is visiting a nursing home, or in other inappropriate places.

Here are the cool rules for playing Gross-Out:

- Adults in charge of the playing area must give their okay to the competition.
- Your grossness may not hurt anyone else or make fun of someone.
- You may not physically hurt yourself by your own grossness.
- The competition is only done at appropriate times and places (remember, not at your aunt's wedding).
- It must be done in fun.
- You must not become too proud of your title as "Grossest of the Gross." Why not? Well, first, it's not necessarily a compliment to win this award! And second, it's not cool to be proud, as Proverbs 3:34 reminds us, "[The Lord] mocks proud mockers but gives grace to the humble."

What fun it is to see a *gracious* gross-out winner, not a proud one!

IS IT COOL to Surf the Net?

Emails! IMs! Websites! Games! Chat rooms! Things to buy! Things to view! Movies! Pictures! Music! There is so much available on the Internet! It's an amazing tool BUT . . . it's one of those things that can be used either for good or bad. The Internet has many great features, but it also has many features that can lead a guy to sin.

Proverbs 21:20 gives some cool advice you can apply to cyber surfing. It reads, "In the house of the wise are stores of choice food and oil, but a foolish man devours all he has." Translation: it's cool to take advantage of the good things God has to offer us — food, oil, and, in this case, the good aspects of the computer. But it's not cool to just eat everything around you. That's not good for your health. Likewise, not everything on the Internet is good for you.

Paul writes in Romans 12:2 and 9, "Do not conform any longer to the pattern of this world, but be transformed by renewing your mind. Then you will be able to test and approve what God's will is — his good, pleasing and perfect will . . . Hate what is evil; cling to what is good."

When you sit at a computer, tuned into the Internet, the world is right in front of you. You have some powerful choices to make. Many times it takes great willpower (that God can grant you) not to click on this or that. That's what not to do, but there are some things you can do, depending on your Internet provider. You could ask your mom and dad to make sure they have set parental controls that limit where you can go and who can get to you. Find an Internet provider that fights spam containing tempting words or pictures. If you really want to chat with someone, there are great Christian chat rooms to visit. Use the blocking controls on your buddy list to keep temptation or hurtful people from contacting you through an Instant Message. It's also cool to choose a screen name or email graphics that tell everyone who sees them you are a follower of Jesus Christ.

Be cool when going online on your computer. It's a jungle out there. And the jungle is just inches in front of your eyes. You have a loving, forgiving God who wants what is best for you and can give you the strength to use your computer and Internet for good, instead of evil.

Surf's up, dude! Happy surfing — in safe waters!

IS IT COOL to Try to Say or Do Something Helpful When Mom and Dad Are Arguing?

This is a touchy one! First, you must remember that your parents are to be respected — always. You probably don't fully understand the situation that has caused their argument. In fact, with many fights or arguments, it's best not to get in the middle of the situation if you don't know the cause of it. A cool wife once wrote in Proverbs 26:17, "Like one who seizes a dog by the ears is a passer-by who meddles in a quarrel not his own." Everybody knows dogs don't like to be picked up by their ears. And people don't like you meddling in their business! You've probably been in an intense "discussion" with someone when another person just walks up and tries to interfere. That doesn't go over very well.

Let's get back to your parents arguing. You'll have to pray about each situation as it comes up. Each time can be different. You may find it best to go to your room and pray for your parents or pray about the topic they are discussing.

But you may also find, in certain situations, that it *is* cool to say something to your parents. If you do, make sure your words show your love and respect for them. It will do no good if you start yelling at them. You can be an example to them. God may want to use you to get them thinking about how they are talking or reacting. God can use the calm, cool voice of a child to bring peace. In fact, Proverbs 12:20 reads, "There is . . . joy for those who promote peace." Make sure peace is your motive if you say something to parents who are arguing. Speak the truth in love (Ephesians 4:15).

For something cool to say, how about gently asking them if they could discuss things when you aren't around. Tell them kindly that it hurts you to see them arguing and ask if they could just think about what they are saying to each other. You may even want to remind them that you love them and that you're going to pray for them and about their problem. Hopefully, if you are respectful with your words, they will respect your concern and in turn respect each other with their words.

Also realize that every relationship, no matter how close people are, will include disagreements. It's the way people *deal* with their disagreements that is important. Anger is not a sin, but it can easily lead to sin, so we must be careful (Ephesians 4:26).

Hopefully, you won't have to deal with this, but if there is ever any physical violence involved in an argument, get help. It's one thing to have a disagreement and to argue; it's very serious when the situation gets violent. If violence happens, get away and find someone to help.

IS IT COOL to Wear Clothes That Have Weird Characters or Sayings on Them?

Clothes with words or pictures on them are like a billboard on the side of the road. They are like advertisements — free advertisements. Sometimes our clothes advertise the company that made them or the store that sold them. Probably plenty of clothes (especially shirts) in your closet, in your drawers, or lying on your bedroom floor have messages printed on them. The message may be in the form of a picture (like one that advertises a band or concert event) or in the form of words. By wearing the message, you're saying, "This product is cool!" or "I agree with what this company or store sells or does" or "This word describes me!"

So, what message are your clothes sending to every person who sees you? Is it a cool message? Is it a message that you would gladly wear in front of Jesus? Do the messages on your shirts and clothes tell others something about your relationship with Jesus Christ? Or do they say that your relationship with the world is much stronger and more important?

Second Corinthians 5:20 reads, "We are therefore Christ's ambassadors, as though God were making his appeal through us. We implore you on Christ's behalf: Be reconciled to God."

We are official messengers, ambassadors, of Jesus Christ. Wow! That's cool! That is *very* cool! But that also tells us we need to consider what message we are giving others by the things we wear. There are shirts with Christian messages on them available to us. Those shirts and other clothing are like big signs, telling others about the love of God in Jesus Christ. We don't have to wear clothes with Christian messages all the time. Just remember that what we wear sends others a powerful message. Our wardrobe and what we buy may change as we remember that being cool in Christ " . . . is the beginning of knowledge" (Proverbs 1:7).

When you wake up tomorrow morning and are deciding what to wear, put on Christ. Wear him in your heart and the entire world will know you are a Christian! Spread the Word! Christ's life, forgiveness, and saving love are "one size fits all."

IS IT COOL to Listen to Music Even If You Can't Understand the Words?

Blagodat Gospodina nasega Isukrsta i ljubav Boga i oca i zajednica svetoga Duha sa svima vama. Did you understand that? What if this entire book were written like that? It wouldn't do most of you very much good. What would be the point in reading it when you didn't get anything out of it? It looks like gibberish. Hopefully, some people using this book do understand what those words say. They're written in the language of the Bosnians. For all most of you know, they could mean something bad . . . or something good. Actually, they are a Bible verse — a blessing — really. The verse translates, "The grace of our Lord Jesus Christ, and the love of God and the fellowship of the Holy Spirit be with you all" (2 Corinthians 13:14).

My point is that it is very cool to know the words of the songs you listen to — what's the point of listening to what might be great music if the words are awful, hurtful, or not pleasing to God? Proverbs 20:12 reminds us that the Lord has made "ears that hear." God has created your ears. Some of you hear better than others — or maybe you listen better. It is cool to think about what we allow to go into our ears, because what goes in our ears eventually reaches our mind! Then we respond to what we put in our mind. What we listen to also tells people about our relationship with God. It's not cool to enjoy listening to songs that make fun of people, use words that are not pleasing to God's ears, include words of hate, make fun of God's gift of sex, or lead us to sin.

Are you thinking, "I can't even understand the words. I just like the music. What does it matter?" Remember, even if you don't know the words, others may. They may also know you are a Christian. They may figure that if you are a Christian and listen to that kind of music, then Christ must think the words are cool too. The words can then be a very bad witness for your non-Christian friends.

Check out the words of the music you listen to. Most CDs have the songs' words printed out. You may also be able to get them online. Ask your friends if they understand the words.

The author of Psalm 40:6 says to God, "You gave me ears to hear you and obey you" (NIrV). As we listen to the things in God's world around us, he asks us to make wise decisions about what we take into our ears and mind. As we listen, we can also rejoice that we hear his voice. He tells us how much he loves us and that he forgives our sins because of what Jesus Christ has done for us, through his death and resurrection! That is music to our ears!

IS IT COOL to Cry?

For crying out loud, there's nothing wrong with crying out loud! Crying is cool *unless* you're using tears (real ones or fake ones) to try to control someone, like a parent or a teacher. You know what I mean, don't you? Let's say you want something but your parents won't get it for you, so you turn on some tears to try to change their minds. You're using tears in a way that God didn't intend for them to be used! (There is an exception to this cool rule. If right now you are flipping through this book and skimming it in the store, I give you permission to cry and carry on until your parents buy it for you!)

For the most part tears are cool. There are sad tears and happy tears. Have you ever had such a serious laugh that you started crying? We usually think of tears at sad times. But God made tears to help us deal with our emotions in all kinds of situations.

When we get hurt, it's natural to cry. You are HURT! If you fall down on the concrete at recess and other kids are laughing, don't feel bad. You know they'd also be crying if they had fallen. They are just being immature and thoughtless. And then, you will remember not to laugh at others when they are hurt, won't you?

We get hurt in other ways, too. If someone says something mean to us . . . that hurts! If someone we know dies . . . it hurts! If our parents fight all the time or get divorced . . . it hurts! It's cool to cry when you are hurting. Tears are a great gift in hurtful times. This gift helps us deal with difficult situations. Trust me on this one! It's all right to cry. Better yet, trust Jesus on this one; he cried, you know. Check out John 11:32 – 36 and Luke 19:41. If Jesus did it, crying must be cool!

I would add that if you feel sad and cry often, say for a couple of weeks straight, please make sure someone knows. You might want to check with a doctor to make sure you're not dealing with something called "depression."

IS IT COOL to Ignore Your Parents' Advice?

Not cool! It's not cool at all to ignore your parents' advice. In fact, the king of cool wisdom wrote in the book of Proverbs, "Stop listening to instruction, my son, and you will stray from the words of knowledge" (19:27). Over and over in the book of Proverbs the wise guys urge, plead, and beg children not to forget the good and godly advice of their parents. One example is found in Proverbs 1:8, "Listen, my son, to your father's instruction and do not forsake your mother's teaching."

It may seem that your parents are part of a totally different world than yours, but they were once your age. They've lived through a lot of stuff and learned a lot of stuff (not to make them sound too old)! They also love you. They're not going to give you advice that's going to hurt you. They want what is best for you (just like your heavenly Father).

I know you might find this hard to believe at this point in your life, but someday you'll probably be giving similar advice to your children. Then you might understand and appreciate what your parents were telling you. But why wait until you're a parent to begin appreciating and listening to the advice of your parents? Be a radically cool kid and start now!

IS IT COOL to Be Cool?

Check out what happens when you accept God's cool words: "for wisdom will enter your heart, and knowledge will be pleasant to your soul. Discretion will protect you, and understanding will guard you" (Proverbs 2:10 – 11). Isn't *that* cool? It is cool to be cool in Christ! It is *extremely* cool to be *humbly* cool in Christ Jesus, your Savior (Proverbs 3:34)! Remember that being cool is based on humility — not on pride or boastfulness. In Ephesians 4:2 – 3, Paul reminds his cool friends, "Be completely humble and gentle; be patient, bearing with one another in love. Make every effort to keep the unity of the Spirit through the bond of peace."

Being cool is all about loving God and others. Those who are truly cool in Christ don't even think about boasting. They just go about their lives serving others in response to God's perfect love for them in Jesus Christ. That's so cool!

IS IT COOL to Ignore or Make Fun of People Who Aren't Cool?

This is an easy one. Let's start by asking you to put yourself in the place of one of those people you have decided is "uncool." Would you like to be ignored, laughed at, or given the label of uncool? Of course not!

God has made us all different. We all have different gifts and talents, hobbies, interests, looks, and sizes. God doesn't make uncool people. The problem is that we all make some uncool choices. (God calls that sin.)

Even if someone looks or acts differently from us, the cool thing is to show God's love, no matter what. Ignoring him isn't the answer. Just saying "hi" to him or listening to his ideas is respectful and cool. The wise one in Proverbs 8:33 reminds his children (and all of us), "Listen to my instruction and be wise; do not ignore it."

A story in 2 Kings 2:23 – 24 shows us that God doesn't think it's cool to make fun of people. The story is about one of his prophets, Elisha, and his encounter with a bunch of young boys who were probably about your age. It reads like this: "From there Elisha went up to Bethel. As he was walking along the road, some youths came out of the town and jeered at him. 'Go on up, you baldhead!' they said. 'Go on up, you baldhead!' He turned around, looked at them and called down a curse on them in the name of the LORD. Then two bears came out of the woods and mauled forty-two of the youths." Yikes! Don't mess with God's chosen people, huh? That's an extreme example, but it does remind us it isn't cool to make fun of or ignore those we think aren't cool. Instead, with God's help, we can look at everyone with compassionate and kind eyes, like Jesus did.

Although we all make some very uncool choices in our lives, I'm very glad that God didn't ignore me. He sent Jesus to die for our sins and to rise from the dead so we can be with him forever in heaven. That's cool!

IS IT COOL to Burp or Make Other Bodily Noises?

This is an interesting (Buurpp! Oh, excuse me!) question. Burping, belching, passing gas, farting, tooting, pooting, and spewing a stink bomb are all names for those bodily noises that can be extremely embarrassing when they happen at the wrong time or even very funny when they happen at the right time! Whatever you call them, they are all a natural part of the function of our bodies. Now, you can do several things to cut down on these noises. Eating or drinking too quickly causes you to swallow a lot of air. When that air escapes through your mouth you have what is known as the burp! That air can also come out of another place on your body, which I'll let you figure out! In the book *The Gas We Pass* by Sinto Cho, we learn that passing gas out of the opposite end from your head can also come from gases found in your large intestine. Those gases are made when leftover food (food that your body doesn't use) is broken down by bacteria, rots, and becomes poop. That's why the gas we pass often stinks! The book also warns that if you try too hard to hold your gas, your stomach may hurt, you might get dizzy, or you might even get a headache. So the author suggests not holding it in, but rather, passing the gas. (Aren't you glad you wondered if burping and other bodily noises are cool?)

So here's the scoop on burping and so forth. In one sense (not scents), it is very natural to pass air or gas out of your mouth or another body part. But, in another sense, you might think of controlling the noises at inappropriate times. If possible, excuse yourself and go into the bathroom if you have to let one fly. As for burping, try not to gulp your drink or food. That will cut down on the unexpected noises. Also, keep your mouth covered, if a burp does sneak up on you.

And don't be a glutton for punishment. Watch what you eat and how much you eat! It's not cool to eat or drink until you pass air and gas or even worse, puke! Proverbs 25:16 has some cool advice: "If you find honey, eat just enough — too much of it, and you will vomit."

In the big scheme of things, these are pretty natural acts, but it is uncool when the timing is wrong. It's covered in what adults call "good manners." And good manners are cool, although sometimes not as much fun as bad manners. Good manners are important. That's the story of the gas you pass! Cool beans, huh? Oops, maybe I shouldn't have mentioned beans!

IS IT COOL to Hate My Classes?

"English is so boring." "When am I ever going to use what I'm learning in Math or Science?" "I can't stand Music Theory class, either. Why do I have to take this class?" Have words like these ever come out of your mouth?

We've all said them at one time or another about some class or subject. But to say a class is useless isn't cool. One of the purposes of an education is to learn a variety of information. No one is ever going to use everything they were taught in school, but you never know how that information may be helpful down the road.

The cool book of Proverbs has some wisdom to throw into the mix. Proverbs 15:22 says, "Plans fail for lack of counsel, but with many advisers they succeed." God has blessed you with many advisers (teachers) in your life. They are knowledgeable in many areas, and they are in your life to help you succeed at whatever God leads you to do with your life.

Take a look at Proverbs 21:5. It reads, "The plans of the diligent lead to profit as surely as haste leads to poverty."

You may not love all the classes you take, but see them as opportunities to grow. Work hard in all your classes. Don't try to rush through them just to get by. That's not cool. And if you really have a tough time working hard in a class, think about the saving work of Jesus — what he went through for you and me — so we could have a seat reserved for us in heaven!

IS IT COOL to Go Off on My Friend When He Makes Me Mad?

Controlling your anger is definitely a cool thing! God says through the writer of the words found in Proverbs 29:11, "A fool gives full vent to his anger, but a wise man keeps himself under control."

It's certainly not always easy to keep your temper under control, but with God's help, you can do all things that are pleasing in his sight (Philippians 4:13). What are the situations where you let your anger run wild? What sets you off? On the other side, are there times when it is okay to be upset at something?

If you feel like you're going to go off on someone, hopefully these cool tips might help. When you feel that you are about to lose your temper . . .

1. Walk away!
2. Turn away from the situation and say a silent prayer.
3. Count to ten. It really works. Give yourself time to calm down. (Sometimes you may even have to count a bit higher!) If you can do two things at once, as you count, ask yourself, "Is this really that important?"

4. If the situation involves other people, talk after you've cooled off.

5. Go into another room, scream, and then come back!

Remember that anger, in itself, is not a sin. God has created us with emotions to deal with life in a sinful world and that is often something to be angry about. But the way we deal with the anger we are feeling makes a huge difference. Be thankful that when Jesus faced the hatred of people, he allowed them to crucify him, so that we can live as his forgiven people . Our Prince of Peace, Jesus, is way cool!

IS IT COOL to Smoke Cigarettes?

Cigarettes are not cool! There is nothing cool about any aspect of smoking. It is bad for our health (it can cause lung, tongue, or mouth cancer, and other diseases) as well as perhaps injuring the health of those around us. In most places, it's against the law for someone your age to buy and smoke cigarettes. Smoking is habit forming. It's a waste of money. It's a waste of time. It is polluting and littering God's world as many smokers throw their cigarette butts onto the ground. It is foolish to do something that has no good results.

We must care about the health of our bodies, which is the temple of the Holy Spirit (1 Corinthians 6:19). And "fear the LORD and shun evil. This will bring health to your body and nourishment to your bones" (Proverbs 3:7 – 8). Don't waste your money on junk like cigarettes; rather, "honor the LORD with your wealth" (Proverbs 3:9).

If kids are trying to get you to smoke, remember the cool words from Proverbs 17:12, "Better to meet a bear robbed of her cubs than a fool in his folly." Don't play the fool! Do play the friend who tries to help others kick the habit! Encourage and help them quit. Then you are *smokin'* in a cool way!

IS IT COOL to Do Drugs So You Can Be Part of a Group or Gang?

Duh! You already know the answer to this one, right? Right? But it's always good to be reminded because you'll probably be tempted with this one in the years ahead or maybe you already have been. Doing drugs is illegal, bad for your health, and a total waste of both money and a cool mind! Yes, drugs change the way you think and do things — in a bad way! Nothing, nada, zilch comes from doing illegal drugs!

The book of Proverbs begins with a warning about the kind of people who are into deadly things (like drugs) "My son, if sinners entice you, do not give in to them. If they say, 'Come along with us . . . throw in your lot with us, and we will share a common purse' — my son, do not go along with them, do not set foot on their paths; for their feet rush into sin . . ." (Proverbs 1:10 – 11, 14 – 16)

People trying to get you to do drugs don't care about you in the least bit! Why would someone who really cares about you give you something that is bad for you? Don't fall for that trick! Rather, get high on Jesus' love for you and his will for your life!

IS IT COOL to Play Practical Jokes on People?

Practical jokes can be cool if:

1. they're done in fun.
2. no one gets hurt (not even feelings) and nothing gets damaged.
3. you would gladly be the one on the other end of the joke.
4. they're jokes your parents would approve of.
5. they're such great practical jokes you could write and tell me about them so I can use them!

The tough thing is that what you *think* may not hurt someone could backfire. It could cause them pain and hurt feelings. It's best to know the person you are playing the joke on very well. That way you know what they might think is funny, and what is not.

Most importantly, make sure you're playing a practical joke in fun and for no other reason. "All a man's ways seem innocent to him, but motives are weighed by the LORD" (Proverbs 16:2).

Have fun, cool one! And may the joy of the Lord be your guide!

IS IT COOL to Compliment Someone?

You are so cool! Your faith is so awesome! You are talented! You're an inspiration!

Those compliments have to make you feel pretty good! So why do so few people give compliments? What's up with that? Complimenting others is cool! Complaining about others is not!

Compliments encourage people. They bring smiles. They're fun! Compliments renew people who are worn out. In fact, Proverbs 11:25 tells us that "he who refreshes others will himself be refreshed."

Start complimenting (but only if you mean it)! Keep complimenting! It's cool! Encourage! It's cool!

IS IT COOL to Complain When You Really Have Something to Complain About?

You've had the flu for three days and you're sick of being sick. Someone is making fun of you and you feel like you can't take it anymore. You don't understand what the teacher is trying to teach you and it doesn't seem to make any sense! Ever felt like screaming? AAAHHHHHH! Life can be tough! You want to complain, and you really have something to complain about. So is it cool to complain?

People don't always handle complainers very well. Sometimes complainers come across as constant whiners. Constant whining isn't cool. What's cool is that God has given us family and friends we can go to and share things that are bugging us.

It's also cool to know that God can handle any complaint. He's big enough to deal with anything. In fact, he's bigger than any problem you might have. The Psalms are full of people telling the Lord what was bugging them. David wrote in Psalm 142:2, "I pour out my complaint before him [the Lord]; before him I tell my trouble." Good plan, David.

Not only is God big enough to handle our complaints, he can send people who care when we're being bugged by something or someone. He can also help solve those big problems. Sometimes his help is in just being there to listen. Just talking to God about things can really help us. God helps in so many ways when we really have something worth complaining about!

IS IT COOL to Want to Win, No Matter What It Takes?

Ecclesiastes 9:10 has some really cool words to say about this question. The cool wise one (most likely Solomon) wrote, "Whatever your hand finds to do, do it with all your might." Give it all you've got! Use your gifts and talents as God has blessed you! It's cool to put everything into working and playing hard. BUT not if winning (a sports game in this example) gets to be more important than your relationship with God; you become selfish; or people are hurt in the process of your work or play. Then it's not cool.

Too many people forget that they wouldn't be able to play well if God didn't bless them with the ability to do so. Some people are so competitive. They get so pumped up that they become very selfish. Everything is about them. Everything is about winning. That is not cool.

Winning a game isn't everything. Working hard and doing your best with a Christlike attitude is very, very cool! Winning the crown of life at the end of life is everything. And Jesus made that possible. Aren't you glad you're on his team? He's the coolest of the cool!

"Commit to the LORD whatever you do, and your plans will succeed" (Proverbs 16:3).

IS IT COOL to Use Words That Sound Like Cuss Words But Really Aren't?

You know it isn't cool to cuss, right? Colossians 3:8 puts us on the cool track about that: "But now you must rid yourselves of . . . filthy language from your lips." But what about those words that sound like dirty words but really aren't? Know something? It's cooler to stay away from those words, too. Many words are used as substitutes for cuss words. One of the big problems is that even if we're not using the actual cuss words, people around us may mistake what we are saying for the bad words. It can be a very poor witness of our Christian faith for the person who misunderstands our words. And, if these substitute words just sound like the bad words, there's no sense in going near them. Check out this: "He who guards his lips guards his life, but he who speaks rashly will come to ruin" (Proverbs 13:3). Serious stuff!

It's not cool to cuss, but it is very cool to choose words that please God. Our words are very important as we grow in our relationships with others. I hope you're cool with God's words of forgiveness for the times when our words have been less than pure.

IS IT COOL to Let Someone Cheat Off You If They Really Need Help with Their Grades?

Cheating is cheating is cheating. There's nothing good about it. So the answer is obvious. It's not cool.

You may really care about your friend and don't like seeing him get bad grades, but you are not really caring for him by letting him cheat off your work. It's not doing him (or you) any good. It's like what Proverbs 16:23 says, "A wise man's heart guides his mouth, and his lips promote instruction." When you stop a friend's cheating, you're helping someone learn more. That's a good thing — a very good thing! "A good man obtains favor from the LORD, but the LORD condemns a crafty man" (Proverbs 12:2). Be a cool blessing! Don't let a cheater, even if he is a best friend, continue in his cheating ways! One day he'll be thankful you stopped him!

IS IT COOL to Be Honest with People, Even If It Hurts Their Feelings?

This is another toughie! We don't always want to know the truth, do we? It can hurt. Let's look at the cool advice from our wise ones. Proverbs 24:26 tells us that "An honest answer is like a kiss on the lips." Let me first say that a kiss on the lips may not sound like a good thing to you at this point in your life, but someday it will! It's meant to be a good thing in this verse!

There's something especially helpful in that verse. Did you find it?

It's talking about an *honest answer*. That must mean that someone asked a question. That's important to remember. It's not cool to just go telling people things that may hurt them. Things like, "I know you didn't ask for my opinion, but I think you are a horrible singer." That's not cool!

But let's say someone asks you, "Do you think I'm a good football player?" What do you say if he's not really a very good football player? First of all, you don't have to lie, but you don't want to hurt his feelings either. Tell him positive things about his football playing. You may also say that he may not be the best football player yet, but he is very good at something else. Being honest is cool, but it is also cool to encourage people in areas where they are gifted.

As you think about this question, put the cool teachings of these two verses together:

Ephesians 4:15: "Speaking the truth in love, we will in all things grow up into him who is the Head, that is, Christ"; and Proverbs 16:13: "Kings take pleasure in honest lips; they value a man who speaks the truth."

IS IT COOL to Be the Class Clown Since It's Good to Laugh and Have Fun?

It is cool to laugh and have fun! God is pro-joy! In fact, Proverbs 10:28 reads, "The prospect of the righteous is joy." Expect joy! Oops, wait a minute. Let's read that again. "The righteous . . ." can expect joy. Sounds to me like it's okay to have fun, enjoy a good laugh, and expect joy if we are doing right.

I've known many class clowns (in fact I see one in my mirror every day)! There are class clowns who are respectful and know when to have fun and when to be quiet. And, like the verse from Proverbs says, those who do right can expect joy! But I've also known class clowns who seem to spend more time in the principal's office than at their own desks.

If you're a class clown, make sure you're the cool kind who loves to see a smile, rather than the frown of a teacher or a principal in a bad mood!

IS IT COOL to Get an Allowance Even If You Don't Work Around the House?

Allowances can be cool. Working around the house is cool. Put those two statements together and you get a double dose of cool. But here's the down and dirty scoop: Don't do work around the house in order to get an allowance. Everyone in the family should pitch in and help around the house with or without an allowance. An allowance is just the cherry on top of the whipped cream!

Your parents don't owe you an allowance. Each family deals with allowances differently. You'll have to respect your family rules. But allowance or not, get cool and do your fair share of the work!

While you're emptying the dishwasher or cleaning up your room, think about these words: "All hard work brings a profit, but mere talk leads only to poverty" (Proverbs 14:23) and "If a man will not work, he shall not eat" (2 Thessalonians 3:10).

IS IT COOL to Read Books Like This One?

Yes! Yes! Yes! Very cool! Very cool! Very cool!
Yes! Yes! Yes! Very cool! Very cool! Very cool!
Yes! Yes! Yes! Very cool! Very cool! Very cool!

Yes! Yes! Yes! Very cool! Very cool! Very cool!

WHY?

"A heart that UNDERSTANDS WHAT IS RIGHT LOOKS FOR KNOWL-EDGE" (Proverbs 15:14, NIrV).

Look for knowledge in God's Word. Look for knowledge in cool books that bring you closer to your Savior, Jesus Christ. Keep reading! And talk about cool, did you know that your name is written in a book? It is — the Lamb's Book of Life (Revelation 21:27)! Talk about cool! Just think, you'll have an eternity to thank Jesus, the Lamb of God and author of The Book, for that honor!

IS IT COOL to Be a Christian?

As a Christian, you know the only way to heaven is through faith in Jesus Christ (John 14:5 – 6). Right? As a Christian who has faith in Jesus Christ keep these things in mind:

- You have the gift of heaven, instead of hell! It's a gift from Jesus for you (Ephesians 2:8 – 9)!
- Your faith and salvation are gifts (Ephesians 2:8 – 9).
- You have forgiveness for all your sins (1 John 1:8 – 9).
- You can have confidence as you go into any situation that God is on your side (2 Corinthians 3:4 – 5).
- You have his peace like you can't find anywhere else in the world (John 14:27).
- Jesus is there for you 24/7, to listen and help (Deuteronomy 31:6).
- He has won the victory over sin, death, and the devil, and he gives that victory to you (1 Corinthians 15:56 – 57).
- He thinks you are so cool that he sings with joy because of you (Zephaniah 3:17)!
- It is so cool that the Lord of all creation has chosen you to be his child (Isaiah 43:1)!
- It is amazingly cool that he calls you to follow him and be his friend (John 15:15 – 16).

Yes! Yes! Yes! It is so cool to be a Christian and live for the Savior who lives for you!

"Trust in the LORD with all your heart and lean not on your own understanding" (Proverbs 3:5).

IS IT COOL for People to Know You Are a Christian?

If someone gave you a million dollars, would you be able to keep that news to yourself and not tell anyone? What if you had a new house to live in? You know you'd have to tell people. You'd be on the phone. You'd tell your class. Everyone would know about the amazing gifts you got.

It's the same way with being a Christian. The gifts God has given each of us are worth so much more than a million dollars or a new house or the coolest electronic gizmos. Can you think of anything better than forgiveness, heaven, and a relationship with the Creator and Savior of the world?

You gotta let it out! The cool proverb writer says, "In all your ways acknowledge him" (Proverbs 3:6). Wherever you are, whomever you are with, no matter how young you are or how old you are, it is cool that people know you are a committed, forgiven, dedicated, humble, happy follower of Jesus Christ! Live out the news! Christians rock because Jesus is the Rock!

IS IT COOL to Go to Church and Sunday School?

You're not getting bored with going to church and Sunday school, are you? What's up with that? That can be the highlight of the week. It *should* be the highlight of the week! That's the place where we get to spend super quality time with our best friend, Jesus. We get to learn more about him, what makes him tick, and why he gets ticked at our sins but continues to love and forgive us. We get to receive God's gifts through his awesome words to us. You know how excited you get when you go online and find out that you have email waiting for you? God has mail for you in the form of letters sent to you through the Bible. He wants to teach us how to get along better with our parents and other family members, teachers, and kids at school.

Church and Sunday school are cool beyond cool! Start thinking of them as one-on-one times with the King of the universe. He comes to you, and you get to respond by worshiping him. Just think how much you'd love to have one-on-one time with your favorite sports player or TV star. This is Jesus we're talking about. He's so much more important than those guys, he isn't even in the same league! And Jesus invites you to spend time with him. How cool is that? Pull up a chair (or a pew or a floor) and listen to the amazing things he wants to tell you. Like the wise one tells his children, "My son, pay attention to what I say; listen closely to my words" (Proverbs 4:20).

You have been invited to hear the Lord God Almighty, up close and in person. Whoa! What an invitation! What an awesome God!

IS IT COOL to Go to War Against Another Country?

We just looked at boxing, which basically has the purpose of hurting someone. So, now the bigger question — what about war? Think that question has me in the corner, up against the ropes, huh? You're right. This is a tricky question.

War in itself isn't cool. Many wars haven't been cool in the least bit. They have destroyed people, homes, and lands for no purpose. Many times, wars were brought on by the self-ishness of leaders who just wanted to show their power.

On the other hand, many of the Old Testament books are filled with war stories. In fact, the Lord *led* the people into many of those battles. When God leads, it's cool. So what's the difference? First, most of the battles you read about in the Bible are a response to a promise God gave his people. For instance, when God promised to give his people the land of Canaan, there were great enemies living in the land. God led his people into war against their enemies, so they could have the land promised to them. Yes, God had a bigger fight on his hands than even those Old Testament battles. His battle was over sin, death, and the devil and he was fighting for us. Because he will do anything to keep his promises, he sent his own Son to win this battle. But to do it, his Son had to die on the cross. The point is that God-led wars are acceptable.

Who knows, we may have future presidents, congressmen, and world leaders reading these words, so let's go to the Bible for help. Proverbs 24:5 – 6 puts it plainly: "A wise man has great power, and a man of knowledge increases strength; for waging war you need guidance, and for victory many advisers."

Leaders who are in great positions of power need to know that knowledge about the *entire* situation will add to their strength. They need to pray for guidance. They need to ask those around them for advice. War should be a last option, used only after seeing that all talks attempting to reason with the leaders of other countries have failed. War shouldn't be motivated by the selfishness of a leader. There are times, though, when people or nations need to be saved from evil leaders. (Hitler is an example.) Each war has to be looked at individually. If a nation does go to war, it must think about what will happen to the innocent people of both lands who could be hurt. Only God truly knows the heart of the leader making the decision about whether or not to go to war. That's why we need to pray that God will give us leaders who trust in him.

IS IT COOL to Be a Leader or a Follower?

Yes . . . to both! Are you a leader or a follower? Do you find that kids go along with your plans or do you end up following the plans of others? God has created everyone with different gifts and abilities. Some have more gifts for leadership, while others do better helping and serving.

There is, however, one kind of follower we all want to be — a follower of the Lord! Proverbs 4:11 – 12 reminds us that the all-wise Lord will lead us: "I guide you in the way of wisdom and lead you along straight paths. When you walk, your steps will not be hampered; when you run you will not stumble."

Maybe God has blessed you with the gift of leadership. If that is the case, remember that children of God are called to be "servant leaders." Never look down on, or put down, others who follow. Leading is hard work and it takes having good relationships with others. Remember the words of God, "The plans of the diligent lead to profit as surely as haste leads to poverty" (Proverbs 21:5).

Whether your gifts are in leading or following, remember this:

- all are called to follow Jesus Christ, the true leader of all.
- both followers and leaders are servants.
- it's cool to follow God's calling for your life.

You have been blessed and will be a blessing to others.

IS IT COOL to Tell Someone You're Sorry?

It's more than cool to tell someone you're sorry. It's super cool! Sometimes it's hard for us to admit we did something wrong. We may throw around our "sorry" word like it was a Frisbee. We go up to someone, put our head down, kick the dirt, and mumble something like, "Uh, sorry, dude." And the other person says, "Whatever, dude!"

What's up with that? James 5:16 tells us, "Therefore confess your sins to each other and pray for each other so that you may be healed." Let's get in the habit of asking someone for forgiveness by saying something like, "Hey _(their name)_, I _(name your sin)_. I want to tell you I'm really sorry for doing/saying that. Will you forgive me?" And we really need to mean it.

Then look forward to the other person saying, "Yes, I forgive you . . . dude!" That's the way it works. Isn't that cool?

It's not only cool to tell others you're sorry but also to ask God for forgiveness. First John 1:9 – 10 reminds us, "If we confess our sins, he is faithful and just and will forgive us our sins and purify us from all unrighteousness. If we claim we have not sinned, we make him out to be a liar and his word has no place in our lives."

IS IT COOL to Act Like It Doesn't Bother Me That My Parents Are Divorced?

Being onstage, in a play, is the only cool time for acting. If something is bugging you, it's bugging you, and you have to deal with it. Would you let mosquitoes buzz around your head all day and act as if they weren't bugging you? Of course not. Then don't play the "everything's-okay-when-it-isn't" game. When you are able to tell other people (including your parents) about your hurts, they'll be able to help you deal with the situation.

Divorce isn't fun for anyone involved. It hurts. It hurts your mom, it hurts your dad, and it hurts the kids. It's okay to say you hurt over the situation. Proverbs 14:10 tells us, "Each heart knows its own bitterness, and no one else can share its joy." You may have friends whose parents are divorced who have similar feelings. They may be able to give you some advice. But no one's situation is exactly the same as yours. Only you know what is truly bothering you and the way it makes you hurt. Wait a minute! We need to change that. Only you . . . and God . . . know because God knows us better than we know ourselves! He knows what bothers us. He knows our secret fears. He knows, understands, and cares about us, and our parents. Talk to him . . . and talk to your parents. It's not cool to act cool when everything isn't cool unless you're in the theater doing a play!

IS IT COOL to Have Piercings?

Ouch! Just thinking about getting a piercing hurts! Let's see if the Bible has anything to say. Genesis 24:22 talks about a man taking out a gold nose ring. Whoa! There are all kinds of talk in the Old Testament about people who had piercings. Here's the scoop: Piercings, like big nose rings, were part of that culture and time. Hmmmm. It seems as if piercings are a part of our culture today. But unfortunately, many of the people piercing their bodies today are doing it for uncool reasons.

For instance, many guys who pierce do it to get attention, to look better or to rebel against their parents who don't want them to have a piercing. Want to know something? The only totally cool piercings were the ones Jesus received when nails were driven through his hands and feet on the cross. Those who understand that this was God's Son who was pierced, and he did it for us, will find out what being cool in Christ is all about. The piercings kids get today don't make them cool — Jesus does!

There are some other serious things to think about. Piercings can cause infection in your body when they aren't done properly and cared for properly. You know, maybe before you get a piercing, you should stop and remember that your body is the temple of the Holy Spirit.

After all this discussion, we can conclude that many piercings (and the reasons they are done) aren't cool. But that doesn't necessarily mean every piercing is uncool. One of the most important things to think about when considering a piercing is how your parents feel about it. Of course, they would have to give their permission to get a piercing anyway because of your age. But when you get older and are considering a piercing, think about the opinions of your parents as well as the thoughts other Christian adults have on the subject.

(By the way, in case you're wondering, the same goes for tattoos! Most people getting tattoos do so for uncool reasons. But there can be serious health risks in getting a tattoo . . . and that is really uncool. The only needles you should ever allow to enter your body are the kind doctors use to help you get healthy!)

IS IT COOL to Pick Your Nose or to Pick on People with Big Noses?

No and no. I guess you're not going to let me get by that easily, are you? I couldn't find anything in the Bible about nose picking. I did find this thought in Proverbs 30:33 that reads, ". . . as twisting the nose produces blood, so stirring up anger produces strife." But I don't think that's anything that can really help us with this subject. So I checked with a couple other sources. First I went to a website that had to do with the etiquette (manners) of a gentleman. Here's what it had to say, under the heading Never Groom Yourself in Public. "This includes picking your nose, chewing your nails and picking your teeth. These areas should only be ventured in private. Committing these acts overtly is a colossal mark of a lack of class" (in other words, picking your nose in public is not cool).

My research also came up with the statistic that more than 90 percent of people surveyed in a recent poll admitted to picking their nose. So, it's not uncommon, but the article said to do it in private. If you're really interested in learning some other facts about this, my research showed that unclean fingers in the nose can result in a cold or other sinus problems. You can transfer the germs on your fingers to your body when you put them in your nose. There's more. If your fingernail cuts the membrane inside the nose, a serious infection could result. So it's cooler (and healthier) to use a tissue instead of your finger. Dig into that thought (oops, maybe I shouldn't have used that word) while we consider the other question. Is it cool to pick on people with big noses?

Come on. You already know that's not cool at all! Don't pick your nose in public and don't pick on other people's noses in public or any other place! No one wants to be picked on and God wants us to respect everyone. Paul writes in 1 Thessalonians 5:15, "Always try to be kind to each other and to everyone else."

Kindness and good manners are cool but picking on others and their noses gets the "Not Cool" award.

IS IT COOL to Think That Girls Aren't As Weird As They Were When I Was Younger?

Just so you know, girls weren't any weirder when you were younger. You just thought they were! As you get older, you'll start to look at girls differently. You may even have a girl as a good friend. Whoa! Girls are cool. They don't even have cooties, like you might have heard!

After God created Adam, he realized something very important. Adam needed a helper. He needed someone to compliment the way he was created. The male needed a female. Genesis 2:18 tells us what the Lord said after creating Adam. "It is not good for the man to be alone. I will make a helper who is suitable for him." If that doesn't answer our question I don't know what does! God thinks males *and* females are cool. He created us, each unique and cool, but important

IS IT COOL to Admit Being Scared of Things?

Most everyone has something (or someone) that scares him or her. There's nothing wrong with admitting it. That's cool.

Some people have what are called phobias. A phobia is a deep, deep fear of something. When a person has a phobia, he or she can't function properly. Here are some real phobias people have . . . and their bizarre names!

- Arachnophobia — fear of spiders
- Arachibutyrophobia — fear of peanut butter sticking to the roof of your mouth
- Didaskaleinophobia — fear of school
- Emetophobia — fear of vomiting (tossin' the cookies, throwing up)
- Lachanophobia — fear of vegetables
- Testophobia — fear of tests

Some pretty wild phobias in that list, huh? Fear is part of our world because sin is part of it. That means fear isn't part of God's perfect plan for us. While we may have fears, we also need to make sure that we aren't scared of something because we're not trusting God. If you page through the Bible, you'll see that people faced some really scary stuff. Many times you'll also find those cool words "Don't be afraid!" Our Lord is telling us that he is in control. He is bigger than anything we could be afraid of. He is there to help and protect us, as well as to build up our faith in him. He reminds us in Proverbs 1:33, "Whoever listens to me will live in safety and be at ease, without fear of harm."

So admitting that you're scared of something is cool. But make sure you run to your Savior for help, knowing you can trust in him for any- thing! Fear

IS IT COOL to Talk on the Phone a Lot, Like My Older Sister Does?

Are you trying to get me in trouble with your sister? Actually, this is an interesting question with several possible answers.

- First of all, having good friends and talking to them is cool.
- Second, we need to realize that God wants us to use our time wisely. The telephone, TV, video games, and computer are all good things, but they can take up a lot of your time. So is spending a lot of time on the phone a cool use of time? It can be — or not. We just need to think about how we use our time and put first things first.
- Third, the fact is, there is also good talk and bad talk. The longer and more often people talk on the phone the greater will be their temptation to gossip. Gossip is not cool. It hurts people in many ways.

Talking on the phone can be cool. But you might want to follow these words to the wise:

- Watch how much time you spend on the phone — don't waste God's time!

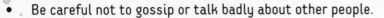

- Be careful not to gossip or talk badly about other people.
- Watch your language.
- Enjoy talking, but first make sure your work is completed (homework, chores, etc.).
- Spend more time talking and listening to your best friend, Jesus, than to others.
- Think about these verses about cool talk:

Proverbs 4:24
"Put away perversity from your mouth;
keep corrupt talk far from your lips."

Proverbs 14:23
"All hard work brings a profit,
but mere talk leads only to poverty."

Proverbs 16:28
". . . a gossip separates close friends."

IS IT COOL to Call Adults By Their First Names?

The answer to this question depends on the situation and what your parents have to say. The main thing to remember is to be cool about respecting adults God has placed in your life. Usually, we show respect to our doctors by calling them "Dr. Andthentheirlastname." You wouldn't go into your doctor's office and say, "Hey, Fred, my man, what's up, dude?" In most situations you would respectfully call teachers Mr., Mrs., or Miss. But there may be situations when your parents allow you to call an adult by his or her first name. That needs to be worked out between you, your parents, and the other adult.

Again, the bottom line is respect. We are called to respect those who are older than we are. A couple of cool verses that remind us of this fact include:

Romans 13:7: "Give everyone what you owe him . . . if respect, then respect; if honor, then honor."

1 Peter 2:17: "Show proper respect to everyone: Love the brotherhood of believers, fear God, honor the king."

IS IT COOL to Play Violent Video Games?

There are some really horrible, gross, destructive, bloody, crude video games. Maybe you've seen them or even played them. God doesn't want us to treat others that way. Even though the character on the screen is just a technological gizmo tearing people's heads off, yelling and screaming, the more we see that rough, cruel stuff, the more we think it's okay. Is that what God wants filling our eyes and minds? Our hands, minds, and brains can do so many cooler things!

Those destructive games (as well as destructive television shows and movies) really do have an affect on people. We want to say and do things that will please God and build up the family of God. That's the cool road to take. Proverbs 13:2 says that "From the fruit of his lips a man enjoys good things, but the unfaithful have a craving for violence." Let's not have fun seeing people tear each other apart. Don't be known as someone who enjoys hurting others, and don't hurt yourself by filling your mind with garbage like this. The cool road is paved with good things. Let's enjoy the ride on that road. See you there!

IS IT COOL to Tell Jokes – Any Jokes?

I don't know about you, but I love to laugh. A great belly laugh is sooooo much fun! So is a snicker and even a smile. Telling jokes can be great fun. One of my favorites is:

Did you hear about the two snakes talking to each other?
One asked the other, "Are we poisonous?"
The other one said, "No, I don't think so."
The first one said, "Whew. I'm glad. I just bit my lip!"

Did that get a laugh out of you? At least a smile? Jokes are cool. Let me rephrase that. Many jokes are cool. However, jokes that make fun of people or the bodies God has created, "dirty" jokes, and those that use bad language are not cool.

You can have great fun with good, clean jokes. People respect you for telling that kind of jokes. People love to smile, and you can help bring on those smiles with a good joke.

But people won't respect you for a bad joke. No matter how smart you are, if you fool around with filthy language and dirty jokes, your brain is useless. Thankfully, it's no joke that Jesus came to forgive us for our sins, including telling bad jokes. With God's help, we want to change what comes out of our minds and mouths. Really! That's no joke! It's just cool news for you and me!

IS IT COOL to Tell Your Mom and Dad You Love Them?

Very cool! No doubt about it! Don't let anyone tell you that it's not. Don't ever be ashamed to tell your parents you love them! Let those words come regularly out of your mouth. Hey, when you go to bed, tell your parents the words, "I . . . love . . . you." Only three little words, but they can make a HUGE difference in your relationship with your parents. We throw around hurtful words so easily. Why do we find it so hard to say these three simple, yet powerful, words?

Don't cave in to other kids' pressure when they tell you it's not cool to tell your parents you love them. That's garbage. How will you learn to express love if you don't begin practicing now? "We love because he first loved us" (1 John 4:19). Not only are we able to love others because God first loved us, we are able to tell them God

loves them too. Jesus is constantly telling us through his Word, his gifts in church, his death, his resurrection, his people, and his world that he loves all of us.

Go ahead, I urge you, beg you, dare you, to say those three little words: "I . . . love . . . you" tonight! I'll bet once you start you'll want to make a regular habit of it. Everyone needs to know he or she is loved. You may know your parents love you, and you may figure they know you love them, but hearing it will make such a difference to them!

Think about these cool passages from the Bible as you start developing the habit of telling your parents (at least once a day) that you love them . . .

Proverbs 17:6
"Children's children are a crown to the aged,
and parents are the pride of their children."

Proverbs 23:24 – 25
"The father of a righteous man has great joy;
he who has a wise son delights in him. May your father and
mother be glad; may she who gave you birth rejoice!"

IS IT COOL to Tell Little Lies When They Don't Really Hurt Anyone?

Who says little lies don't hurt anyone? Is there such a thing as a "little" lie? Lies are going to hurt someone . . . period! They hurt you and they hurt others. Here's the quick answer: No, it's not cool to tell little lies. They hurt people.

The cool, wise writer of the words in Proverbs 16:13 tells us, "Kings take pleasure in honest lips; they value a man who speaks the truth." You may be thinking, I don't spend much time around kings! Oh don't you? What about the King of Kings, Jesus? He spends all his time with you.

Earthly kings need to be surrounded by people they can trust. Their decisions affect many people. Earthly kings value truthful people, not liars. The King of Kings is the same way. His decisions affect our lives forever. Thankfully, he decided to die for sinners (even liars), so they could change their ways. He let himself be hurt so we wouldn't hurt others by dishonest words.

With that thought, lie down in your bed tonight and sleep peacefully. The King of Kings, Jesus, won't leave your side. That's the truth! Cool, isn't it?

IS IT COOL to Smell?

Yes, it's cool to smell! That's why God gave you a nose! Smell burgers grilling. Smell cookies baking. That's cool. BUT what's *not* cool is to smell, as in "Phew! You stink!" Big difference. God gave us noses for smelling, but the rest of our bodies are made to take care of, including making them smell good.

I know it's hard to smell good after playing basketball for two hours, or working in the yard with your dad for what seems like 20 hours!

Guess what? Your body is changing, and that means you're going to sweat more, which means you're going to stink more. You're going to have bad breath sometimes. Your clothes are going to need to be washed more often.

You're going to have to do things differently. So:

- Take a shower (or bath) every day. Clean up with soap, not just water!

- Wash your hair every day. Make sure you have shampoo you like, so you'll use it.

- Brush your teeth and floss. Get toothpaste you like.
- Raise your arm and rub some deodorant over that weird part of your body!
- Don't keep wearing the same clothes unless they are washed between wearing — that includes shirts, socks, pants, and especially underwear! And put your dirty, stinky clothes in the laundry room so they don't stink up your room.
- Smile, and the world will smile back!

You'll be surprised how much more people will enjoy spending time with you and being close to you, when you take care of the body God has put in your care!

One final thought . . . Proverbs 20:9 reminds us that no one can say, "I have kept my heart pure; I am clean and without sin." Even though we don't want to admit our lives are dirty with sin, they are. Thankfully, we have a Savior who wants us to be perfectly clean through his forgiveness.

IS IT COOL to Want to Be Rich?

It would seem that being rich would solve all your problems, right? That would be so cool, wouldn't it? Well . . . not necessarily! Yes, some advantages come with having lots of money, but you'd be surprised how many problems also come along with those riches! One very big problem is that riches make it easier for us to fall away from God because they tempt us to think money is the answer to all our problems, instead of God.

There are also many wrong ways to get rich, and it is tempting for us to try to get rich in one of these wrong ways. What is cool is to know when to say "No!" to tempting offers. God may bless you with lots of money some day, who knows? But you're going to see and hear many ads on TV, radio, and the Internet that tempt people to get riches without earning them. Staying close to God will help you say no to those tricky schemes.

If you are one day blessed with lots of money, think about all the good things you can use it for: helping your church grow, sending missionaries, being a missionary, helping the poor and homeless, supporting a family who doesn't have much money, and lots of other neat things.

Proverbs 23:4 – 5 says, "Do not wear yourself out to get rich; have the wisdom to show restraint. Cast but a glance at riches, and they are gone, for they will surely sprout wings and fly off to the sky like an eagle."

There will always be rich people, poor people, and those somewhere in the middle. The apostle Paul said something super cool in Philippians 4:11 – 12, "I have learned to be content whatever the circumstances. I know what it is to be in need, and I know what it is to have plenty. I have learned the secret of being content in any and every situation, whether well fed or hungry, whether living in plenty or in want."

Do you want to know Paul's secret of contentment? It's really not a secret anymore. The secret to being content, whether you are rich or poor or anywhere in between, is to complete-ly trust in Jesus Christ. Knowing him and trusting him gives you peace. You don't have to worry about the past or the future. All is cool with Jesus in charge. So don't worry about whether you will be rich or not. Relax! All is cool with Jesus!

IS IT COOL to Get Married and Have Children?

At your age, you're probably not thinking much about getting married! You're probably even wondering why we ask the question. Maybe you are looking forward to getting out of school and getting a job. Once in a while you might even think about what it would be like to be married. First of all, enjoy being a kid! But also remember that when you are much older, it will be cool to get married and have children. Marriage is a gift from God. The cool, wise one writes in Proverbs 19:14 that "a prudent wife is from the LORD." Getting married and having children is one of God's plans for many

people. He told Adam and Eve, "Be fruitful and increase in number" (Genesis 1:28).

Some of you may wonder because the marriages around you (maybe even in your own home) may not be very cool if you ever want to get married. Think about these things:

- Marriage is a very important step. Start praying right NOW that one day God will send you just the right wife, one who will love both the Lord and you. Pray for that person's faith — starting now!

- If you think there isn't such a thing as a good marriage, you are wrong. Even if the marriages you see aren't happy, yours could be different. It could be very happy. That's why it's so important not to rush into relationships. Finding the right girl will probably take some time.

- Learn to respect girls and women. Don't look down on them or talk down to them. Don't make fun of them. Respect them.

- Forgive those around you (like your parents) who haven't given you the best example of a Christian marriage. Christian marriages consist of two forgiven sinners who need to rely on God's love to help them learn how to love. Husbands and wives need to learn to forgive, and to grow in God's love together.

IS IT COOL for Parents to Punish Their Children?

Ever meet a kid who liked to be punished? Probably not. No one likes to be punished, but God says it is an important part of growing up to become a man of God. (In other words, God thinks it's cool.) Correcting, disciplining, and punishing when necessary are acts of love. Proverbs 13:24 says, "He who spares the rod hates his son, but he who loves him is careful to discipline him."

It is important to know that not all the punishment you receive will be done out of love. That's because all parents are also sinners living in a sinful world. That means, unfortunately, parents sometimes take out the pressures of their day on the people they love the most — usually family. That's not cool. It's easy for parents to yell at their kids when they are tired, worried about the pile of bills to be paid, or frustrated for some other reason. But it's not love.

When God talks to parents about correcting their children, he says it must be done in love. Here's an example: Imagine you had a dog that kept running into the street. You wouldn't let him keep doing that because you love him. You'd try to train him to stop. If you didn't, your dog would soon be roadkill. Or what if your dog kept going poop in your room? Would you just let him keep on like that? Duh. Of course not.

You'd train him, correct him and if that didn't work, you'd punish him! You love your dog, and you love your room. But you won't love the way your room will start to smell if you don't train him.

In the same way, your parents don't want you to get hurt. They don't want you to smell up your life or the lives of others either. So they offer appropriate training and if you deliberately refuse to be trained, then there will be appropriate punishment. Even though it's not fun, in the long run your life will be blessed if you are corrected . . . in love.

Here are a couple more cool verses about this subject:

Proverbs 29:15 and 17

"The rod of correction imparts wisdom, but a child left to himself disgraces his mother . . . Discipline your son, and he will give you peace; he will bring delight to your soul."

Proverbs 22:6
"Train a child in the way he should go, and when he is old he will not turn from it."

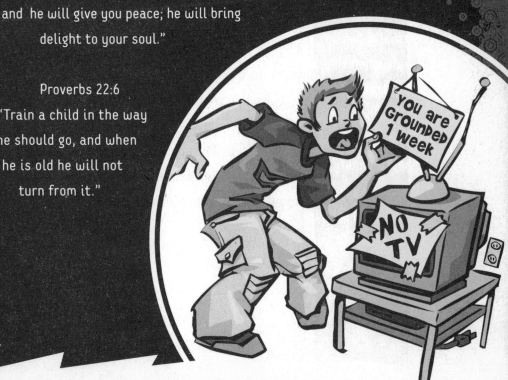

IS IT COOL to Pray for Bad Things to Happen to People Who Act Mean?

It is tempting to pray for bad things to happen to mean people, but it's not necessarily cool. You can find examples in the Bible (especially in the Psalms) of people asking God to destroy their enemies. But if we look to the Bible for a cool answer, we'll find that we are to pray for our enemies (in a good way) and we are even to love them! We are to pray for those who persecute us (Matthew 5:44). These are tough things to do! Proverbs 30:32 adds these words: "If you have played the fool and exalted yourself, or if you have planned evil, clap your hand over your mouth!"

No doubt, it's tough to put our hands over our mouths when we want to say things to hurt people who are mean. It's tough not to pray against them. But what we need to do is let God be God. He'll take care of things. Sometimes the way he takes care of things surprises us. At times, we won't like the way he works. But we need to let him be God — a God who is in control.

If you know someone who is mean, here's a short prayer you may want to pray:

Dear Father in heaven, I'm praying to you in Jesus' name about (fill in name). I don't understand the way he thinks, speaks, or acts. I don't know what has made him so angry or mean, but you do. Forgive me, first of all, for any sinful thoughts I have had about him. Change the way I look at him. If possible, use me to help him know you and your way of life. Keep my prayers pure. Thanks for loving me, even when I am unlovable. I even want to thank you for leading me to be able to pray for my enemies. I love you, Lord. Amen.

IS IT COOL to Be the Best Student in My Class?

When you read this question, I bet you were thinking of the best student as the one with the highest grades. Am I right? Or were you thinking that the best student is the one who is most popular? Or maybe the one kids think is the coolest.

Let's look at it a different way. The best students are those who have respect for the Lord. That's where real brains and knowledge begin. That is the beginning of cool in Christ. Starting at this place changes the way you look at grades, the way you respect teachers, coaches, pastors, friends, and even enemies. Proverbs 1:7 says, "The fear of the LORD is the beginning of knowledge, but fools despise wisdom and discipline."

Respect (fear) for the Lord changes everything. It even changes the way you think about being the "best" student. You become humble and try to be the best in the eyes of God, not in the eyes of other kids. If you are the 'best' in your class in some aspect (grades, sports, music, art, etc.), you know there is no way it would be possible without God's help. You give him thanks instead of looking for praise from others. You realize that you will do the best you can when it comes to schoolwork and grades. What others think of you doesn't matter as much as what God thinks of you. And you know he thinks you're the best. Now that's cool!

IS IT COOL to Get a C on My Report Card? ("C" Stands for Cool. Right?)

Wouldn't it be cool if a "C" on your report card really did stand for "Cool"? On the other hand, a C isn't such a bad grade . . . unless you know you could have done better. A C is an average grade. Some people are using all the gifts God has given them like intelligence, good study habits, close attention in class, good note-taking, and the best grade they can get is a C. If that's the case, then a C is cool. But if students aren't using the brains God gave them, if they are just coasting along

and not studying like they should, taking very poor notes in class, and they don't pay attention, then a C isn't cool. They could have done much better.

As you study, keep Proverbs 3:21 in mind. It reads, "My son, preserve sound judgment and discernment, do not let them out of your sight." God has blessed everyone with different gifts. Use whatever gifts he has blessed you with to the best of your abilities — and to his glory!

And don't forget this truth: You're not getting an average grade in his grade book! He's grading you based on Jesus' life. That's a perfect score! Cool!

IS IT COOL to Let Someone Else Take the Blame for Something I Did?

The teacher leaves the room and the class starts to go crazy. Paper airplanes fly. Kids throw their pens trying to knock the planes out of the air. You pick up a kickball and figure it will do much more damage to the paper airplanes than pens. That's right. It not only knocks the plane out of the air, it also knocks half the things on the teacher's desk onto the floor! OOPS! Not cool. You rush back to your desk, hoping no one saw who threw the ball.

And things are going according to plan. People hear the crash and turn around, but you are just sitting there calmly (or at least you look that way)! Then your teacher returns. You're praying like crazy. Suddenly you realize you're praying you won't get caught. Is that right? The teacher makes the mistake of guessing who did it, and the usual class troublemaker gets blamed. Whew! Was that close. Now, is that cool? You know the answer, don't you? Do you think the other kid is going to take the blame when he didn't do it? Do you think he *should* take the blame? Obviously not. It would be so easy to just sit there and be quiet. But that wouldn't be fair . . . or cool. Proverbs 16:8 adds these cool words: "Better a little with righteousness than much gain with injustice."

There's only been one time in history when this situation was cool. It happened a couple thousand years ago when Jesus took the blame for us. He also took the punishment for us. He died in our place so we could live forever with him. We sure didn't deserve that! But he did it anyway. Isn't it mind-bogglingly cool to be loved like that? Whew! Thank you, Jesus, for saving us!

IS IT COOL to Share Secrets?

Know a good, juicy secret? Oh, it's so hard to keep it. But it's not cool to tell a secret that someone shared with you. It can tear apart friendships, ruin relationships, break a trust, or hurt someone's feelings or reputation. In a cool way, Proverbs 11:13 tells us, "A gossip betrays a confidence, but a trustworthy man keeps a secret."

If you feel you can't keep secrets, tell the person who is sharing before he or she shares something with you. If others do choose to share something private with you, be honored they feel they can trust you. But also make sure that the secret isn't just gossip about someone else — that's not cool!

Be very honored that someone cared enough about you to share the secret that Jesus gave his life for you! Now, go tell someone else. That's one secret God doesn't want us to keep to ourselves.

IS IT COOL to Save My Money While My Friends Are Buying Things?

It's fun to have money to buy things, but it's also cool to save some of it. You don't have to be a magician to know how to make money disappear. One trip to the arcade, sports store, movies, mall, batting cages, or corner store and "POOF!" it's gone! Why does it seem like it takes forever to get money, and no time at all to lose it?

Because everyone seems to want money so badly, it can be tempting to try to get it in ways God wouldn't be pleased with — like gambling, get-rich-quick schemes over the Internet or TV, stealing, or so many other ways. It's cool to make and save your money the old-fashioned way — getting paid for odd jobs, saving your allowance, or getting money from relatives and friends on birthdays and other occasions and holding onto it.

Proverbs 13:11 tells us that "Dishonest money dwindles away, but he who gathers money little by little makes it grow." This verse also could be used to remind us to save money the same way — little by little. Ask your folks to help you open a bank account. Then you'll even get interest on your money! It may not be much, but every little bit helps. It's also very cool to give God part of the money you get. He's the one who made it possible for you to have money in the first place. Another cool thing is to thank your parents whenever they spend money on you. They're working hard to make sure you have the things you need. They're glad to share with you, but it's so cool to be thankful and not just expect them to get you everything.

Enjoy the blessings money can bring, but don't LOVE money. First Timothy 6:10 says, "For the love of money is a root of all kinds of evil."

You are rich through the inheritance Jesus has for you! That's something you can bank on! Jesus' interest is in savings — saving you forever! Now that's cool!

IS IT COOL to Ask My Mom, Dad, or Other Adults for Advice?

Sometimes it's hard for kids to talk to adults about serious things. Maybe it's a guy kind of thing. You might have questions about your faith. You might be having problems at school with other kids, teachers, or homework. Or maybe you know you should talk to an adult about some temptation to sin you're struggling with. What do you want to talk to your parents or another adult about? Or should we change that question to . . . what do you *need* to talk to your parents or another adult about?

Whatever it is, know that it is cool to talk to an adult you trust. Maybe that adult is your parent, a grandparent, a teacher, your pastor, or someone else God has placed in your life. You may think that adults can't relate to what you're going through. But remember that adults were also once your age. Plus, they have lots of experience. They've made decisions that have worked for them, and they've made decisions that didn't work out so well. They will help you avoid repeating their bad decisions. Adults appreciate it when kids come to talk to them. They love to share the wisdom with which God has blessed them during their lives. They think it's cool to give advice!

Here's a cool verse that reminds us it is cool to ask adults for advice: "He who walks with the wise grows wise, but a companion of fools suffers harm" (Proverbs 13:20).

IS IT COOL to Take Care of My Pet?

I consulted with three experts on this subject, and here are their answers:

Expert One: "Woof! Arf! Arf! Woof!"

                    (Translation: Yes! It's very cool!)

Expert Two: "Meow. Meow. Meow. Meow. Purrr."

                    (Translation: Yes! It's cool, cool like a cat!)

Expert Three: "A righteous man cares for the needs of his animal"

                    (Proverbs 12:10).

   I think it's unanimous! Three out of three experts agree that it is very cool to take care of your pets!

IS IT COOL to Be a Loser?

YES! YES! YES! It's cool to be a loser!

Huh? you say. Hold on a minute. Let me explain. There are actually two answers to the question. The "Yes-it's-cool-to-be-a-loser" answer is based on the cool words of Jesus in Mark 8:34 – 35, "If anyone would come after me, he must deny himself and take up his cross and follow me. For whoever wants to save his life will lose it, but whoever loses his life for me and for the gospel will save it."

Get it? It's cool to be a loser in the sense of losing your life for Jesus and his gospel, the Good News. So what does that mean, to lose your life? It means that Jesus Christ is going to come first in your life. It means you'll have to take yourself out of the number one spot and let Jesus have control. It means giving up your sin. Being a "loser" in that way is cooler than cool! It's the way of Jesus. It's answering his call. It's living for Jesus, who lives for you.

If you've lost your life in Christ's life, everything has changed, including the answer to the question, "Is it cool to be a loser?" If you've lost your life in Christ's life, it's impossible to be a loser! All who lose their lives for the sake of Jesus Christ are winners. They have the victory! You are a victor, not a loser. How cool! How awesome! What love! What a Savior!

IS IT COOL to Be a Boy?

I've seen them. You've seen them. I'm talking about the shirts and posters that read, "Girls rule!" Well, they're wrong! God rules! Boys and girls are equal in his sight! And whoever God has created you to be is way cool! So yes, it's very cool to be a boy!

Don't doubt that fact. And please don't doubt the rock-solid fact that God loves you, as a boy (who is quickly turning into a cool man of God)! Your awesome God created you. He knew you before the creation of the world. He saw you before your parents did. He has great plans for you (Jeremiah 29:11). Check out this cool, cool, cool passage from Psalm 139:13 – 18: "For you created my inmost being; you knit me together in my mother's womb. I praise you because I am fearfully and wonderfully made; your works are wonderful, I know that full well. My frame was not hidden from you when I was made in the secret place. When I was woven together in the depths of the earth, your eyes saw my unformed body. All the days ordained for me were written in your book before one of them came to be. How precious to me are your thoughts, O God! How vast is the sum of them! Were I to count them, they would outnumber the grains of sand."

WHOA! Cool truth! Amazingly cool! You are cool in the sight of God. You are a cool boy! You are a cool young man, growing to be a man of God. Rejoice in God's love for you in Jesus, and grow in his truth and salvation. And with God's help and grace (undeserved love), you will become more and more pleasing and in favor to others! (Check out Luke 2:52 one more time.)

Cool! Cool! Cool!

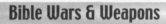

2:52 Soul Gear™ Books–

Action, adventure, and mystery that only a boy could appreciate!

Laptop 5: Dangerous Encounters

Written by Christopher P. N. Maselli
Softcover 0-310-70664-5

Laptop 6: Hot Pursuit

Written by Christopher P. N. Maselli
Softcover 0-310-70665-3

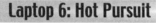

Laptop 7: Choke Hold

Written by Christopher P. N. Maselli
Softcover 0-310-70666-1

Laptop 8: Shut Down!

Written by Christopher P. N. Maselli
Softcover 0-310-70667-X

The 2:52 Boys Bible–
the "ultimate manual" for boys!

The 2:52 Boys Bible, NIV
General Editor Rick Osborne

Based on Luke 2:52: "And Jesus grew in wisdom and stature, and in favor with God and men," this Bible will help boys ages 8-12 become more like Jesus mentally, physically, spiritually, and socially–Smarter, Stronger, Deeper, and Cooler!

Hardcover 0-310-70320-4
Softcover 0-310-70552-5

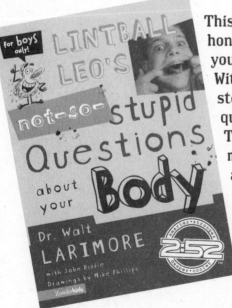

We want to hear from you. Please send your comments about this book to us in care of zreview@zondervan.com. Thank you.

Zonder**kidz**.

Grand Rapids, MI 49530
www.zonderkidz.com